DISNEY'S
ANIMAL
KINGDOM®

Fittingly, Disney's Animal Kingdom Park opened on Earth Day, 1998. Celebrating animals that ever—or never—existed, the Park focuses on the issues facing them through unique, live-action adventures; breathtaking attractions; and entertainment spectacles. In order to ensure that the different "lands" were authentic, designers traveled to remote communities and wildlife preserves, collecting thousands of pictures, artifacts, and mental images to give their concepts realism and authenticity. This resulted in a complete scenario of life in the wild arranged for the well-being of the animals and the amazement of the guests passing through or walking along the edge of forests and grasslands. In this "new species of theme park," you can venture out on safari across the African savanna to encounter freely roaming wildlife, whisk back to the Cretaceous period to save a dinosaur from extinction, or travel up a Himalayan mountain to get a glimpse of the legendary yeti.

Oasis

Oasis is a verdant, walk-through entrance that creates a buffer from the noisy, hard-surfaced world outside as it begins the foray into the refreshing world of green nature. As its name suggests, its purpose is to welcome, refresh, and relax visitors in a cool, natural place where they can encounter animals with welcoming, gentle characters. Ringed by vine-covered crags, the paths of Oasis lead into a miniature world filled with streams, shadowed grottoes, flowering glades, and tumbling waterfalls that fill the air with a cooling spray. Rhinoceros iguanas, babirusa, hyacinth macaw, and swamp wallabies are encountered in pools, lawns, and meadows. The animals here, which include brilliant macaws, miniature deer, and shaggy anteaters, have exotic colors, beautiful shapes, and odd forms, representing the rich diversity of animal life.

The emphasis is on nature, as animals live in an idyllic garden untouched by the hand of man. The benches, lights, and other architectural details are based on the Arts and Crafts design movement of the early twentieth century, where the colors and textures of nature were utilized to create an organic aesthetic.

Disney's Animal Kingdom by the Numbers	
1	million square feet of rockwork in the Park— twice the volume of Mount Rushmore
2	new elephant vocalizations that have never been reported before
4	million plus trees, plants, shrubs, ground covers, vines, epiphytes, and grasses that were replanted from every continent except Antarctica
$4\frac{1}{2}$	tons of food per day needed to feed all the animals
27	million gallons of water in Discovery River
40	different species of invertebrates in the Park
100	and more acres of savanna, forest, river, and rugged terrain in Kilimanjaro Safaris
110	approximate number of plant species in the Park that have never been grown in North America before
260	types of grasses
300	and more species of animals in the Park, consisting of more than 1,500 birds, mammals, reptiles, invertebrates, and amphibians
500	and more acres in size—the largest of the four Walt Disney World parks
850	species of trees
1,359	number of recycled plastic milk jugs used to make a bench for the Park
2,000	species of shrubs
3,000	species of trees, plants, shrubs, vines, grasses, ferns, etc.
5,000	specimens of fish
10,000	and more samples of animal droppings that lab technicians have analyzed since the Park opened
30,000	number of bugs the Giant Anteater can eat in a day
40,000	worms per week ordered to feed some species of animals
80,000	crickets per month ordered to feed some species of animals

Discovery Island

The colorful Discovery Island is a hub that serves as a departure point, literally connecting the bridges that span Discovery River, which lead to adventures in all of the other realms in Disney's Animal Kingdom. It is also the home of the towering icon of the Park—The Tree of Life. Carved and painted animals can be found on all the buildings and structures in the area, expressing the depth of humans' love for animals and celebrating the creatures' beauty, uniqueness, and interconnectedness.

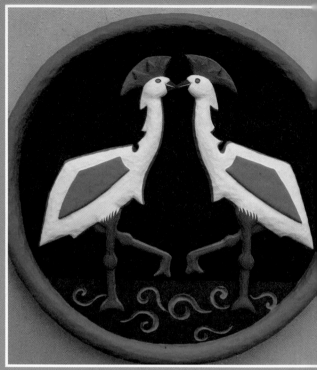

Discovery Island Trails

Surrounding the root system of The Tree of Life are the Discovery Island Trails. This soft, landscaped garden of trees, shimmering pools, and grass-fringed foliage is inhabited with small primates and marsupials, as well as a host of colorful birds, including ducks, flamingos, cranes, and cockatoos. Drawn from all over the world, the animals represent no particular continent or eco-system, but are chosen instead for their amazing diversity of form, beauty, and playful behavior. The animals range from the largest of their kind: Galápagos tortoise, saddle-backed stork; to the smallest: cotton-top tamarin; to some of the strangest: red kangaroo, ring-tailed lemur. The otter exhibit, contained in a 67,000 gallon tank of water, can be seen from an otter's eye level underwater as well as from above.

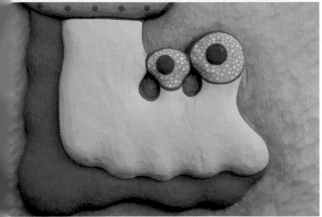

Animal Adornment

The design motifs on the shops at Discovery Island illustrate various categories of the animal kingdom in a colorful, whimsical way. The Beastly Bazaar features animals that spend much of their time in water: fish, turtles, otters, bears. Creature Comforts is decorated with spotted or striped animals: zebras, tigers, giraffes, bumblebees. Notice the ladybug lamps outside. Island Mercantile showcases animals that migrate: butterflies, geese; or those that work: beavers, donkeys. Disney Outfitters' animals travel in herds: elephants, rhinoceroses.

The restaurants display a similar approach to design. The several rooms at Pizzafari offer a large menagerie of groupings of ornamental animals: peacocks, parrots; upside-down hanging animals: bats, possums; animals that carry their houses: snails, kangaroos; nocturnal animals: owls, raccoons; and animals that use camouflage: leopards, deer, polar bears.

Flame Tree Barbecue pairs animals in a predator/prey relationship: ants and anteaters, spiders and bugs. Note that the tables are decorated with the prey animals, and the chairs you sit on are adorned with the predators!

The Tree of Life

Rising up from the lush garden set in the midst of Discovery Island, The Tree of Life represents not just vegetative nature but life itself. It is a celebration of all living things and their place in the great circle of life. The Tree of Life rises over the island, crowning it with a dense cover of translucent leaves that shift and sigh with the breeze. Worked into its gnarled roots, mighty trunk, and sturdy branches is an intricately carved, swirling tapestry of animal life: dolphins, lions, monkeys, insects, bats, and elephants, which appear to magically emerge from within. The message of the Tree of Life is that of the diversity of life—a many-branched community of living creatures that arose from a single ancestor. The Tree of Life and its location symbolize a belief that Nature and natural systems are at the center of the scheme of life.

While its look was ultimately inspired by a diminutive bonsai tree observed by Imagineers, building its support structure required an engineering approach similar to those used in building huge offshore oil rigs. After the platform and frame were set in place, the armature of the branches was positioned, and the entire edifice was layered with structural foam. The foam was coated in concrete embedded with steel mesh, and that in turn was covered with the plaster the artisans carved the animals into. Finally it was painted, all in a process that took more than two years.

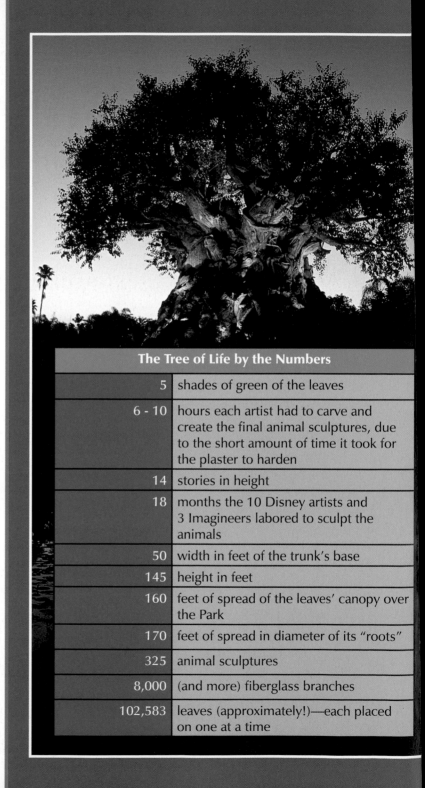

The Tree of Life by the Numbers	
5	shades of green of the leaves
6 - 10	hours each artist had to carve and create the final animal sculptures, due to the short amount of time it took for the plaster to harden
14	stories in height
18	months the 10 Disney artists and 3 Imagineers labored to sculpt the animals
50	width in feet of the trunk's base
145	height in feet
160	feet of spread of the leaves' canopy over the Park
170	feet of spread in diameter of its "roots"
325	animal sculptures
8,000	(and more) fiberglass branches
102,583	leaves (approximately!)—each placed on one at a time

It's Tough To Be A Bug!

Among the roots of The Tree of Life is the home of The Tree Of Life Repertory Theater, which has been packing audiences in for years with hit shows such as *Beauty and the Bees*. The latest show at The Tree of Life will guarantee you'll never look at bugs the same way again. *It's Tough To Be A Bug!*, the most elaborate spectacle that the Repertory Players have mounted yet, is hosted by Flik from Disney•Pixar Animation Studios' *A Bug's Life*. It's a creepy, crawly, and funny 3-D musical revue that points out just how tough it really is to be a bug. And remember: Please refrain from buzzing, stinging, pollinating, or chirping throughout the presentation.

Camp Minnie-Mickey

In an area modeled on an Adirondack mountain retreat, Camp Minnie-Mickey is a place of true character. Mickey, Minnie, Goofy, Donald, and Pluto, among others, have gone for a restful vacation, where they meet new friends who join them at this fun wilderness resort. Passing sculptures of Daisy leading Donald's nephews, Huey, Dewey, and Louie, on a hike; and Mickey and Pluto fishing in a stream, visitors to the camp walk along greeting trails to rustic, wooded pavilions, where they can say hello and get an autograph and a hug from these beloved characters.

Pocahontas and Her Forest Friends

Is there really only one animal that can save America's forests and the animals that make their homes there? Native American legend says there is. But which one? At Grandmother Willow's Grove, the elderly teacher advises, "You must ask the animals." So Pocahontas sets out to find the answer, with the assistance of the little sapling, Sprig. This intriguing story is told in a tree-shaded grove where live animals, native to North America, make cameo appearances onstage to display their natural traits and demonstrate how they can help. Live animals, including a raccoon, a skunk, a possum, forest doves, and porcupines help Pocahontas discover that the only animals who can save the forest are—you guessed it—humans. Based on characters from the film *Pocahontas*, the stage show uses the music from the film as a sound track.

Festival of the Lion King

Festival of the Lion King tells the story of a traveling band of performers who visit Camp Minnie-Mickey and use music and dance to convey the important role each one of us plays in the "great circle." The spectacle combines the pageantry of a parade with the excitement of an African tribal celebration. Four giant rolling stages move in from two directions as performers and props sail through the air over the heads of the audience during the opening chorus of "I Just Can't Wait to Be King," which is performed by singers in tribal robes. Innovative animated figures and acrobatics are showcased as the center stage doubles as a trampoline for a troupe of "flying monkeys" during a rendition of "Hakuna Matata." Stilts are worn by warriors performing the dark "Be Prepared," and high-wire aerialists dressed as giant birds hit a high note in the love duet "Can You Feel the Love Tonight," which literally soars. The show comes full circle with a chorus of "The Circle of Life," followed by the audience's participation in a rousing version of "The Lion Sleeps Tonight."

FESTIVAL FACTS

🦁 The hosts of the show are Kibibi (Princess), Kiume (Strength and Masculinity), Nakawa (Handsome), and Zawadi (Gift).

🦁 A twelve-foot-tall Simba sits on Pride Rock, while Timon and Pumbaa cavort around a jungle area. Completing the "circle" are a towering giraffe and a playful pachyderm who spouts water from his trunk at "Elephant Falls."

🦁 The four audience sections are warthog, elephant, giraffe, and lion.

🦁 Fifty performers wear approximately 136 costumes during the show.

Africa

Jambo! Hello! Expeditions into the wilds of Africa begin at the edge of a typical wildlife reserve in the coastal town of Harambe, with its bustling marketplace and whitewashed walls. Airy arcades provide shelter and atmosphere with eating and shopping places along the way. Along the shores are the fishing nets and dhows of the seaside village's inhabitants. The Swahili-inspired architecture features hand-plastered buildings with partially exposed coral-rock substructure and walls weathered by sand and rainstorms. Corrugated metal and thatched roofs predominate.

In this city on the edge of a wilderness, travelers come to experience incredible adventures. Kilimanjaro Safaris is a journey through a wild savanna in the heart of Africa, where lions, giraffes, and zebras roam freely. The Pangani Forest Exploration Trail is a walking tour through a luxuriant forest preserve that is home to a troupe of lowland gorillas, a village of frisky meerkats, and Nile hippopotamuses. The Wildlife Express Train travels to Rafiki's Planet Watch for a backstage tour and the closest encounter you can have with animals in the Park.

The architectural scale of the landscaping in Africa and the other lands at Disney's Animal Kingdom is suppressed to allow trees to "overshadow" the buildings; overall building height is limited. When possible, trees native to Africa were transplanted to the site, including the maringa trees with their sausagelike seedpods at the end of Mombasa Marketplace/Ziwani Traders. Some trees are man-made, others were found on the site and reshaped to resemble African foliage. For example, oak trees that flourish in Florida have been pruned to resemble signature African trees, such as the flat-topped acacia. The largest tree replanted in the Park is located in Harambe village; it tipped the scales at ninety tons—that's equal to the weight of sixteen elephants.

Harambe

Harambe is a realistic, contemporary representation of an East African coastal village poised on the edge of the twenty-first century. In this new tourist mecca, visitors can eat, shop, and meet some of the village residents. Harambe, which means "coming together" in Swahili, may be weathered by time but it is rising to the challenges of the new millennium. Signs for the Harambe Fort, erected in 1420, are seen directly across from an advertisement for the Kivvko Computer Training Center. Above Mombasa Marketplace/Ziwani Traders are the district offices of the Harambe/Malind Survey Office. The Mkubwa House was built in 1781 and restored in 1992.

The town's created "history" is apparent in the stone remnants of the old city and its fortress walls, which are still embedded in the pavement. Roots stick up through fractures in the walkways, and buildings are sorely in need of a paint job or a plastering of their crumbling walls. A bench with the words "Urhuru 1961" (Urhuru means "freedom") speaks to a break with its colonial past, though a British influence can still be seen in mailboxes and signs.

While informed by the towns of Lamu, Shela, and Mombasa in Kenya, the Imagineers who designed Harambe chose not to copy a single street or marketplace, instead capturing the essence of a busy coastal city. They collected African artifacts and distinctive signs to give it authenticity. Thirteen Zulu craftsmen from Kwazulu-Natal, South Africa, were brought in to construct the authentic reed-thatched roofs on the buildings. Fifteen trailer loads of thatch came with them.

Tusker House Restaurant

Patrons pass through the blue doors of Tusker House Restaurant (which advertises "The Best Food in East Africa") into a rustic yet elegant open-air restaurant decorated with maps, safari schedules, and animal skulls. Native crafts, including baskets, instruments, and artwork, adorn its various rooms and are displayed under a canopy of drapery hanging from the ceiling. The "second floor" sports colorful fabrics and weaving tools. Tucked into one corner is an advertisement for the masks, beads, and earrings sold at the "Jorodi" shop.

The middle section of Tusker House is known as the Safari Orientation Center. A detailed map of the Harambe Wildlife Preserve is displayed. Also hanging on its walls is apparel from several African cultures, including those for a Kumba and a Turkana woman, a Kumba Celebration Costume, and raiment for a Maasai Warrior and Maasai woman and a Lamu coastal man. At the Kivulini Terrace, there's waterside seating for diners, near where the Kisiwa boat resides. Next door, the Dawa Bar in the "Hoteli Burutika" offers a relaxing outdoor area from which to people-watch.

In a back area of Tusker House is an informative chalkboard that translates important Swahili words into English.

KWA KISHWAHILI	ENGLISH
Jambo	Hello
Karibu	Welcome
Tafadhali	Please
Asante	Thank You
Kwa Heri	Good-bye
Nyani	Baboon
Nigiri	Warthog
Hapana Kuweka Magar	No Parking
Tafadhali Ucha Mikono Ndeni Ya Gari Mara Zote!	Please keep your hands and arms inside the vehicle at all times!

Kilimanjaro Safaris

At the top of Harambe's main street is the most successful of the town's several photo-safari companies: Kilimanjaro Safaris. (Kilimanjaro, the name of the highest peak in Africa, is an extinct volcano in Tanzania.) Operating for nearly three decades, Kilimanjaro Safaris is the front-runner in offering safe and affordable animal-viewing safaris. Equipped with a fleet of sturdy, open-sided "Tembo" (Swahili for "elephant") vehicles built for tourism (weighing ten tons each without passengers), the company operates on the Harambe Wildlife Reserve, which is public land preserved as a national park and administered by the town. Safari tour companies like Kilimanjaro provide welcome jobs, taxes, and benefits to the town. The Wildlife Reserve wardens also appreciate having extra eyes to report any evidence of poaching.

Kilimanjaro's company motto is: "When it comes to Safaris, we go WILD!" The company hires and trains its drivers to offer a high level of information about the lives of Reserve wildlife. Since the Reserve is a wild habitat with continuously shifting populations of animals, drivers never know what wildlife they might encounter and need to be ready to describe many different species. The employees of the company, who come from all over Africa and even as far away as the United States, are concerned about the welfare of Africa's wildlife, both as a valuable natural resource and as one of our planet's last, magnificent vestiges of free-ranging animal populations.

Under the shelter of a gnarled baobab tree, safari patrons board an open-sided lorry after watching a videotaped welcome from Wilson Mutua, the Wildlife Reserve's head warden and an experienced pilot on the lookout for poachers. The safari will travel over water-filled ruts and bumpy trails as it explores 110 acres of characteristically East African terrain: moist upland forests, curving rivers cut through sandy banks, dry brush forests, open grassy savannas, and eroded granite hills called kopjes.

Okapi and black rhinos lounge by the Bongo Pool, and hippos enjoy a cooling mist at the base of a waterfall as the truck makes its way to a bridge that crosses over lounging crocodiles. In the grasslands, giraffes, sable antelopes, and Thomson's gazelles forage for food. The ostriches there could easily outrun the truck. Rounding a bend, a mandrill baboon family resides in a rock formation, while another turn reveals a herd of elephants traveling to their watering hole. A flock of pink flamingos gracefully perches nearby as white rhinos and warthogs relax at another watering hole. A high rock formation reveals sunning lions.

The trip takes an adventurous turn as the driver picks up a radioed request—the pilot can't locate the baby elephant, Little Red. Then Wilson spots poachers in the area. The truck races off to catch them. Fortunately, a follow-up report reveals that the poachers have been caught and Little Red is safe as the adventure ends.

Pangani Forest Exploration Trails

Located inside the Harambe Wildlife Reserve is the Pangani Forest Conservation School & Wildlife Sanctuary, a joint effort of the citizens of Harambe and international conservation groups. This research center, dedicated to studying and preserving the lives of endangered local wildlife, provides a self-guided walking trail that allows visitors to get close-up views of East African mammals, birds, fish, and reptiles, which are too small or too difficult to observe from a safari vehicle. Set in a lushly wooded valley (Pangani is Swahili for "place of enchantment"), wildlife biologists and research students gather from across Africa and around the world to do field research on lowland gorillas and other rare creatures. The school's staff and volunteers have built a series of animal-viewing blinds, cutaways, lookouts, and other structures filled with equipment and notes telling the stories of the animals' lives. The research structures are rustic and spartan, offering a brief glimpse into the world of animal field studies with its attendant paraphernalia of microscopes, biological specimens, meticulous notes, and concern for endangered species.

The first observation area contains Okapi, the only known relatives of the giraffe; Stanley (also known as Blue) Cranes; and yellow-backed Duikers, members of the antelope family. Duiker is African for "diver," which accurately expresses the way these animals dive into the forest undergrowth when in danger. Entering a field house, visitors are drawn to a colony of naked mole rats, burrowers with a highly organized society similar to that of a bee colony. The field house exit leads to an aviary housing rare and exotic birds—coffee-colored jacanas, carmine bee-eaters, and bearded barbets.

One trail away from the bird sanctuary are a series of natural habitats, including an area that houses some highly animated meerkats. Another direction leads visitors to a large, glass-walled viewing area where hippos can be seen swimming a lap or two in a 96,000-gallon tank of water. Weighing anywhere between one and five tons, these buoyant creatures create a natural ballet more fascinating than their tutu-wearing cousins in *Fantasia*.

As visitors continue along a leafy, verdant trail, two troupes of lowland gorillas can be observed in a bamboo jungle replete with waterfalls and streams. A family consisting of a silverback male, two females, and a few infants (who are known to spend time watching the humans through a glass-walled viewing area) is on one side of a swaying suspension bridge and a bachelor troupe of silverback males is on the other.

WE DO NOT INHERIT
THE EARTH FROM
OUR PARENTS –
WE ONLY BORROW IT
FROM OUR CHILDREN.

Rafiki's Planet Watch

Rafiki's Planet Watch is the nerve center of the Park and the hub of its global conservation efforts. This fun-filled activity area combines Disney characters, interactive technologies, and hands-on experiences designed to stimulate a desire to know more about what's happening to the animals of our planet. The attraction places an emphasis on current, positive news of work being done by zoos, communities, and individuals around the world to save animals and wild places.

Wildlife Express Train

On the outskirts of Harambe stands a 1920s-era railway station, with high windows, an airy ceiling, and a tin roof. The Eastern Star Railway has named the train that runs to Rafiki's Planet Watch the Wildlife Express. The train consists of five open-air carriages, a puffing steam engine, and a locomotive that is a replica of a 1926 Byer-Peacock 2-4-2T steam "loco" built in Manchester, England, and commonly operated in East Africa. As Wildlife Express leaves Africa, it begins a backstage tour of animal support areas, chugging past the cheetah, white rhinoceros, and African elephant night houses before arriving at its destination.

Habitat Habit!

Habitat Habit! is a series of exhibits along the path leading from the Wildlife Express to Conservation Station that offer helpful hints on how we can bring the idea of conservation to our own backyards. Methods of dealing with trash and water elements and responsible pest control are demonstrated for enviromentally minded visitors. Eco-sensible animal feeders and houses are exemplified in butterfly gardens, bat houses, and an environment for cotton-topped tamarins, as well as ponds and fountains that showcase amphibian- and avian-friendly techniques.

Affection Section

The Affection Section provides a place to have a close encounter with small domestic animals such as goats, sheep, and pigs. But in a twist, this petting yard features rare breeds of these animals from across the globe. Performers on an outdoor stage in the Affection Section present informative and fun shows where visitors can interact with the animal care staff.

OPEN YOUR EYES TO THE WORLD AROUND YOU

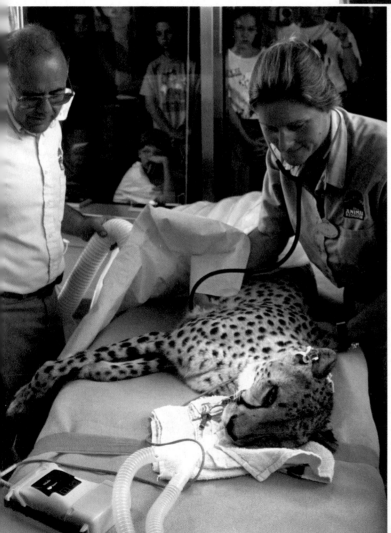

Conservation Station

Brightly colored animal sculptures peer from the top of Conservation Station. This building hosts shows and activities about saving animals, conserving the land, and preserving future resources, and offers visitors a window into the training, feeding, and care of animals. Visitors can engage in a variety of interactive video and computer shows that answer questions about wildlife and even let them speak to world-famous conservationists. Live animal exhibits and an in-depth look into veterinary nutrition and research programs all provide informative perspectives on wildlife issues.

• In Song of the Rainforest, the sounds of a rain forest surround listeners as Grandmother Willow speaks to the multilayered existence of this endangered resource.

• Rafiki's Planet Watch Video is an interactive video that provides information on endangered animals, hosted by the wise baboon.

• EcoWeb is a computer resource for information from and about conservation organizations around the world.

• The Eco Heroes interactive video kiosks allow viewers to interact with world-famous biologists and conservationists.

• Animal Cams provide a way to view the Park's animals in their backstage homes through their Guest-operated video cameras.

• Animal Health and Care teams shows the Park's research, veterinary care, and food preparation teams in action.

Asia

Namaste! Tashi Delek! As visitors cross the bridge to Asia, they enter the mythical Kingdom of Anandapur (a Sanskrit word meaning "place of all delight"), filled with the crumbling yet beautiful ruins of the ancient village, its temples, and even a maharajah's palace. The land's rain-forest habitat and striking murals further cultivate the ambience. Tigers, Komodo dragons, and giant fruit bats live among the palace ruins. Two massive monument towers under restoration, one Thai and one Nepalese, provide an ideal setting for two families of gibbons to create a hooting racket that echoes throughout the land while they play. In the distance, a snowcapped mountain beckons adventurers to an exciting new adventure.

Asia in Disney's Animal Kingdom depicts the look and feel of lands where ancient lifestyles, modern development, and endangered wild habitats create a compelling story about animals today. It offers a condensed segment of Asian peoples, landscapes, and animals from the tropical shores of Indonesia and Thailand to the hill country of Nepal and northern India. The Tiger Tree near the entrance exemplifies the way nature and civilization interact over time, an important motif in this land. The statue has been overtaken by a tree hung with ribbons left by travelers to Anandapur. The ribbons represent their prayers and have been left to disintegrate in the wind lest they be invalidated. Bells indicate an answered prayer.

At the base of Asia's mountains, in a lush, enchanting setting, adventurers can enjoy unforgettable experiences that challenge the spirit and open the heart. The Maharajah Jungle Trek is a breathtaking walking journey through the lush home of myriad bird and animal species, including magnificent Asian tigers. At Kali River Rapids, rafters voyage on the turbulent Chakranadi River for a wild, wet ride through a jungle habitat threatened by illegal logging. Expedition Everest takes riders into the pristine lair of the legendary yeti on a perilous trip through the Himalayan mountains aboard a runaway train.

Flights of Wonder

The first and only attraction in Asia when it opened with the Park in April 1998, Flights of Wonder features exotic birds of all types presented on the Caravan Stage, a crumbling fort reminiscent of structures found along the Silk Road. Here we meet a bird-handler trainee who has much to learn about how to treat wildlife. More than twenty bird species are discussed or presented here, and their skills, such as responding to visual or auditory cues, hunting, and eating, are showcased. Through their natural behaviors and displays of free flight, the birds themselves help teach observers that nature should be respected as well as enjoyed.

Expedition Everest

Legend holds that high in the Himalayan mountains lives an enormous creature that haunts the remote forests and fiercely guards the land, long considered sacred . . . and forbidden. Belief in this protector has kept thousands of acres of land pristine. The region around Mount Everest is such a place. . . .

The village of Serka Zong (Fortress of the Chasm) at the mountains' base consists of several buildings, including the Yeti Palace Hotel, the Shangri-La Trekkers Inn and Internet Café, and Gupta's Gear, all reflective of a contemporary Himalayan village where ancient traditions and modern trends combine. Adventurers flock to Norbu and Bob's to book their Himalayan Escape (there and back on the flying yak!) and to Tashi's Trek and Tongba Bar for last-minute supplies. Colorful flags emblazoned with symbols loop from building to building, inspired by Himalayan prayer flags that send thoughts and prayers into the wind. The Yeti Museum, which was previously a tea warehouse, has maps, artifacts, and photos presenting the legend, lore, and science of the yeti to visitors. A warning at the exhibit's conclusion has been posted by curator Professor Pema Dorje: You are about to enter the sacred domain of the yeti, guardian and protector of the Forbidden Mountain. Those who proceed with respect and reverence for the sanctity of the natural environment and its creatures should have no fear. To all others—a warning—you risk the wrath of the yeti.

Boarding a refurbished tea plantation train at the Anandapur Train Service, travelers begin their journey to the lowlands at the base of Mount Everest in the Himalayas. After passing bamboo forests and small shrines, the train, known as a "steam donkey," ascends the mountain at a steep angle, passing through a tunnel carved from rock beneath an ancient fortress. Inside, a monumental mural depicts a wild-eyed hairy creature—the yeti, guardian of Forbidden Mountain. After crossing a chasm on a creaking train trestle, the train suddenly screeches to a halt before tracks that are twisted and bent. Releasing the brakes, the train continues its journey—backward! The chilling howl of the yeti can be heard echoing off the surrounding mountains as the train finally stops in a large cavern. The yeti is spotted again, but unfortunately it spots your train, which leaps forward. Racing on, the train descends to the base of the mountain, then spirals upward and back inside, speeding through mountain caverns and icy canyons, before an inevitable showdown with the protector of this hidden realm.

Expedition Everest by the Numbers	
2	trips by Imagineers to China and the eastern Himalayas for research
3	stories in the Yeti Mandir building
10	species of trees in the landscape
80	foot drop when the train descends from inside to outside
110	species of shrubs planted
900	(and more) bamboo plants in the lowlands area
1,000	yetis carved into the Yeti Mandir
1,800	tons of steel used in the mountain structure
2,000	handcrafted items from Asia in the props, cabinetry, and architectural ornamentation
2,000	gallons of stain and paint used on the rock work and village

Kali River Rapids

Anandapur is set somewhere in the floodplains and lower foothills of the Himalayan mountain range. Born from the melting snows of the mountains, the Chakranadi River flows down from the hills and through a dense jungle toward the coast, creating a rich habitat for both animals and people. Chakranadi is a Sanskrit word that means "River that Flows in a Circle."

A walk through Anandapur reveals many colorful signs advertising mountain trekking, animal viewing, and river rafting. These represent the trend toward eco-tourism that helps fuel Anandapur's economy. One of the oldest and best known of these adventure-travel companies is Kali Rapids Expeditions, a river-rafting group that takes tourists out on the Chakranadi's white-water rapids. Founded by a local woman, Manisha Gurung, the raft company is named after the most thrilling stretch of the river—the Kali Rapids—which is named in turn for the many-armed Hindu goddess who represents the destructive forces of nature—forces that change, break, and reshape the world.

Rafters first travel through a huge bamboo tunnel, where they're enveloped in a jasmine-scented mist as the raft climbs upriver into the headwaters. A sweeping waterfall fills the view, and a giant, carved tiger face appears from behind the falls. Gliding beyond the wondrous rain forest and temple ruins, the raft emerges suddenly from the bamboo thicket, and the sweet jasmine aroma is lost to the acrid smell of burning wood. Fires are burning, trees are falling, a habitat is destroyed, and the lush, pristine lands are endangered—a constant threat in Asia. As the raft twists and spins through the river, travelers encounter illegal loggers from the Tetak Logging Company (tetak means "to chop"), who have destroyed the landscape, leaving behind burning timbers and a mud-caked truck that has slipped down an embankment. A tangled arch of burning logs looms ahead as the raft rushes toward a fiery doom.

Disaster is narrowly avoided when the raft drops down a rocky canyon of waterfalls and continues through turbulent waters. Surprises emerge around every turn, including more abrupt drops into the churning waters. As the debarkation site comes into view, two playful elephant statues make sure that everyone in the raft is thoroughly soaked by the end of the adventure.

Maharajah Jungle Trek

The Kingdom of Anandapur bids you welcome to the Maharajah Jungle Trek. In the ancient remains of a sultan's palace, this animal sanctuary exemplifies how nature has taken over what man once mastered. Painted or plastered walls have eroded due to wind and water. Tree roots have burst through the floor, and architectural details have been scraped off by branches. The largest monitor lizard in the world, the Komodo dragon, which can grow up to twelve feet long, basks nearby in the sun. Playful gibbons; shy Malayan tapirs, which are relatives of the rhinoceros; Eld's deer; and other animals roam freely among the luxuriant vegetation, lotus pools, and shaded ruins.

The four faded murals seen before and after the tiger-viewing rotunda depict legends of the royal hunt from ages past and also represent the history of the palace and the four kings who resided within it. Each of these men had a different relationship with nature and the beasts in his kingdom. The first king established the area as a royal hunting reserve in 1544, building a hunting lodge that was soon surrounded by the small village of Anandapur. The second king is shown enjoying the material wealth that his power and riches brought him. After a time of war, the third king proved to be a conqueror who defeated his enemies and restored the palace. Finally, the last king completely fled the ravages of man and nature. It took over 120 artists more than five months to create these murals.

Giant fruit bats fly above the bat cliffs of Anandapur, where visitors can watch them through large, open windows as they fly or hang from trees and the cliff's rocky walls. The giant flying fox is the largest bat in the world, with a wingspan reaching more than six feet. The smaller Rodriguez bat is found on tiny Rodriquez Island near Madagascar in the Indian Ocean.

Majestic Asian tigers safely lounge on the tiles of a once-beautiful fountain, taking up residence near a place where they were once hunted. Vibrantly colored birds have taken over a decayed ballroom as their aviary. The domed shrine in the ruins of this great hall houses a wooden pavilion that displays "portraits" of some of the species in residence, such as the Indian Pygmy Goose and fruit doves. Amid the quiet tranquility of the area, the melody of the white-rumped shamas may be heard. This bird is considered to have one of the most beautiful birdsongs in the world. Smaller shrines in the area contain food offerings from the villagers.

DinoLand U.S.A.

You don't need to go to the ends of the earth—you're here now! Celebrating our fascination with dinosaurs, this quaint, family-oriented "fossil park" grew out of the bone-rich diggings discovered here sixty years ago. On the current site of Restaurantosaurus, an amateur fossil hunter made the first find at what was then a fishing lodge. Banding together with some scientist friends, he bought the land to continue his paleontological pursuit. Restaurantosaurus has served as a visitor's center, a museum, the first incarnation of The Dino Institute, and a student clubhouse. Over the years, a stream of bone-hunting professors and grad students attending The Dino Institute have built and inhabited a series of wooden structures, tin Quonset huts, and streamliners that give the land its nostalgic look. The Dino Institute is a research facility built to serve as a discovery center and laboratory dedicated to uncovering the mysteries of the past. The attending grad students do their best to offset the stodginess of the Institute's faculty by irreverently adding "osaurus" to buildings and signs, when they're not leaving lawn chairs on the roof of their dormitory or shooting arrows at the water tower.

A fifty-two-foot tall, eighty-foot-long Brachiosaurus has been reassembled to create the land's magnificent gateway Olden Gate Bridge. DinoLand U.S.A. is located along Diggs County Highway, US Route 498. (Why 498? It's the month and year of the Park's opening!) Make no bones about it—you'll dig this place.

THE DINO INSTITUTE

EXPLORATION · EXCAVATION · EXULTATION

The Boneyard

The original dig site discovered in 1947 is still being worked and studied by the fossil hunters of The Dino Institute. Bones, fossils, and reconstructed skeletons are everywhere. There are so many fossil remains here that the ongoing excavation process has itself become an attraction known as The Boneyard, where visitors can slide down chutes, climb rope nets, and prowl through caves in a discovery oriented play maze. Budding paleontologists can even dig up the remains of a ten-thousand-year-old Columbian mammoth in one of the biggest and best sandboxes of all. The "bones" in The Boneyard were cast from real dinosaur bones found in such places as Utah's Dinosaur National Park and then reproduced in a plastic cement that looks and feels real.

Chester & Hester's Dino-Rama!

Those dino-maniacs, Chester and Hester, are two forward-thinking and enthusiastic entrepreneurs who have made a fortune mining the past. Chester and Hester turned their rural house and gas station into a gaudy, dinosaur-themed souvenir shop (currently featuring a "Going-Out-of-Existence Sale") and opened an old-fashioned carnival of bright string lights, amusing attractions, midway-type games, and classic pop tunes to capitalize on visitors to the nearby Dino Institute.

Chester & Hester's Dino-Rama! is a throwback to the roadside attractions that appeared from the 1940s to the 1960s in the Southwest, with exaggerated architecture such as the Cemento-saurus at the entrance to Midway Games and whimsical entertainment venues in a cretaceously crazy fun fair atmosphere that offers "Rides of Extinction."

Primeval Whirl

This spinning "crazy mouse–style" roller coaster zips through a time warp to a prehistoric era in a race against extinction on a twisting maze of tight loops, hairpin turns, and sudden dips. Colorful vehicles whirl past flying asteroids and corny depictions of dinosaurs before a meteor shower spins the cars into the gaping jaws of a giant dinosaur fossil. Everyday objects straight from the kitchen and garage, such as egg timers, clocks, car parts, and bicycle reflectors, create these seemingly homemade time machines.

TriceraTop Spin

Sixteen green, three-horned, chubby dinosaurs move up, down, and around on TriceraTop Spin. A hub-and-spoke ride, it magically becomes a giant spinning top that ultimately reveals another dinosaur inside. As cartoon comets and glowing stars whiz by, this ride is a chance to see a dino "soar" in a whole new way.

Dinosaur

DinoLand U.S.A. grew enough to need expanded research headquarters, so The Dino Institute was built. With more space and resources available, its paleontologists focused their attention on the riddle of the dinosaurs' extinction. One theory is that a huge meteor smashed into the earth sixty-five million years ago, causing the dinosaurs' disappearance along with its global catastrophic effects. This theory can now be investigated firsthand as The Dino Institute has acquired the rights to a time-traveling vehicle which is the current star of the Institute's presentation—Dinosaur.

Visitors find that they are to become part of this daring adventure. Renegade scientist Dr. Grant Seeker is determined to bring back a live dinosaur from the Cretaceous era, and he's sending the Institute's guests into the past to rescue an iguanodon from the meteor's destruction. Boarding their "time-rover," passengers pass through "time compression" to emerge in a dense nighttime forest, lit by the baleful glare of the approaching meteor. At first, all goes well, in spite of a swooping pterodactyl and a hungry alioramus.

Things get worse when a carnotaurus, a giant carnivore, pursues the passengers as they bump,

slither, and skid their way through the primeval terrain. Seconds before the meteor is due to hit, the vehicle becomes trapped and the carnotaurus closes in for the kill. Rescue comes in the form of the very dinosaur the team was sent to retrieve. As they roll safely back into the Institute and exit the time port, sharp-eyed time travelers might get a glimpse of a hitchhiking iguanodon on the television monitors.

Finding Nemo - The Musical

The undersea world that charmed audiences in the Disney•Pixar Animation Studios film *Finding Nemo* comes to life in a unique musical stage show at the Theater in the Wild. "Finding Nemo–The Musical" immerses the audience in the story of Marlin and Nemo, the overprotective clown fish father and his curious son, through a dazzling production that combines puppets, dancers, acrobatics, and animated backdrops. This production marks the first time Disney has taken a nonmusical animated feature and transformed it into an original musical production.

The newly enclosed Theater in the Wild becomes a magical undersea environment through innovative lighting, sound, special effects, and the theatrical puppetry of Michael Curry, who designed the richly detailed character puppets seen in the Broadway version of Disney's *The Lion King*. The original songs, which include "In the Big Blue World" and "Go with the Flow," were written by Kristen Anderson-Lopez and Tony Award–winning composer Robert Lopez. Principal characters, such as Marlin, Nemo, and Dory, are represented by live performers operating larger-than-life puppets. Supporting characters, such as Nigel the pelican, and the huge cast of marine life—sea fans, coral, and an acrobatic hermit crab—are realized in a diverse array of puppetry styles that include rod, Bunraku, and shadow.